Your copy:
№ 1 of Four

To Dave —

Happy.
Birthday
2009 —
have
Hope you
a Writerly Year —
Nicky

Façade
Nicky O'Neill

A Skrev Press Pocket Book

Published in 2007 by SKREV PRESS:

SKREV PRESS
41 Manor Drive
HEBDEN BRIDGE
HX7 8DW
skrevpress@ukfsn.org
www.skrevpress.com

First Edition 2007
ISBN 978-1-904646-49-5
IMAGE — *Splitting Hairs*

NICKY O'NEILL | HARLOW

... ✍

Nicky O'Neill (Harlow)[1] indulges her dubious artistic passions in several ways: by writing, painting, taking photographs and performing mediocre impressions of Joyce Grenfell for her long suffering family. She teaches Creative Writing for the Open university and lives in Hebden Bridge with her two daughters and her beloved paramour, David, who is, as it happens, another writer. This short collection comes after years working in both paid and unpaid capacity in what can loosely be called 'the arts', an acrimonious divorce and too many of the afore-

---

[1] Former married name

mentioned paramour's home-made wines.

Other Titles by Nicky O'Neill

Nicky has written two novels: **Meru**, Castle of Dreams Books, 1996, **Russian Dolls**, Insignia Press, 1999 and one collection of short stories, **Wasted** Skrev Press, 2004. She also had short stories published by Route (most recent, 'Candle', Skin collection 2007), Leaf Books, Bloodlust.com, MsLexia, Skrev Press's Text Bones, and two novellas published by Barley Books 2000. Her play, **Mary the Maid of the Inn**, was performed by Yorkshire Equity in 2005. Nicky is also a visual artist. Two self-illustrated collection of short stories will be published later this year: a Gothic collection, A Cure For Eating Disorders; and a minging collection of realist shorts, The Famous Author Who Came Between Us. She is currently working on a new novel, Amelia and the Virgin.

Acknowledgements

Nicky wishes to thank the following magazines for first publishing the stories collected here: -

Venus in Furs Whereof We Cannot Speak ... Critical Theorists Can't Keep Their Gobs Shut; Zigzag

More Than A Woman Rhotacism is a Pain in the R

He Ain't Heavy Farewell My Lurcher

Down the Chip Shop Spiders & Flies

Flesh Make it New

Nicky wishes to especially thank the Journal, Texts' Bones for taking a risk publishing some of the more riskier material and to the heated approbation of Zigzag readers, one of whom said of **Venus in Furs**:-

"What an impressive piece of writing this was. Wry, humorous, cynical, intelligent. Gripped me from start till the end. Sometimes made me laugh out loud:)"

CRUMBLING EDIFICE

. . . ✍

§ 1 Façade

§ VENUS IN FURS

. . . 🖎

L et me put you in the picture, frame
my case. The art world is phoney,
thick with intrigue, dense with medioc-
rity. The cult of the artist as artwork is
so established that even the critics never
question the validity of the artefact, only
the quality of the hype. There is no mention of merit, of talent, of message any
more. There is only entertainment and
shock; a temporary stimulation of the sen-
ses, enough perhaps to provoke a conver-
sation at a cocaine-fuelled dinner party,
no more.

I know this for I am Mr Aitch, the
celebrated fine art dealer.

Take the phenomenon of Humbert and

Smiley. Both are artists in my stable, polar opposites. Humbert is a mincing dandy of diminutive stature and filthy predilections; a man for whom the term cottaging could have been invented. Smiley, by contrast is a heterosexual giant — both medical and mythological. Seven foot tall with a shock of ginger hair and teeth like tombstones, he idolises women but remains single. Humbert and Smiley are a moveable feast. They are one and the same man. If their respective publics know of this, they choose to look the other way. Their reputations precede them and no one has yet seen them leave.

Now I shall choose my palette, block in the background with some ambient colour.

Yesterday, I was in the Café des Arts, sipping a latté, having just sold one of Humbert's dreadful daubs for over ten K. There weren't many people in, a couple of students, the usual selection of disaffected art lecturers and some retro poet, whose unrhymed verse seemed tailored to a 70s Variety Club audience, a man for whom punk was far from dead. Anyway, there was I, in my favourite seat, looking out over the old part of town, quite taken up with thoughts on how I was going to spend the money, when who should walk in but old Smiley.

Now, Smiley is the jewel in my otherwise tawdry little crown. He is the goose that lays the golden egg, and consistently,

not like Humbert, whose overpainted delv-
ings into the homosexual underworld usually result in the art establishment's de-
rision and the tabloid bosses' orgasms.
His use of human (his own) excrement,
semen, nose pickings, and latterly blood
from his own burst haemorrhoids tends
to put off all but the most ardent gay
collector.

I prevaricate, Smiley tapped on my shoulder, disturbing me from a reverie so deep
it took a couple of minutes for me to
recognise him. He does, I must impress
upon you, take a lot of trouble with his
appearance, not like the Mohicaned poet,
to make himself stand out from the crowd,
to make a statement. Quite the reverse.

Smiley goes out of his way to blend in, to assume the appearance of wallpaper in whatever social surrounding he chances to find himself. Today he was sporting a motheaten duffel coat and a pair of faded jeans with frayed edges. His ginger locks were smoothed down onto his head in an oddly fashionable marcelle wave. He wore a shark's tooth earring and a pair of horn-rimmed spectacles.

I was in a good mood. Ten thousand pounds up, my only worry which debt to pay off first. I waved Smiley over to my table, intent upon ordering a bottle of Claret, some cigars, maybe an appe-tiser to celebrate, but Smiley had other ideas. He, at odds with his name, did not look happy in the least.

'What can I do you for?' I asked, jovially when the hapless giant had arranged his legs under two tables. 'Wine? Beer?'

Smiley ordered two pints of best Belgian lager. He paid for it himself. Feeling slightly put out that my generosity had been spurned by one whom I knew to be far less wealthy than myself, I went ahead and ordered a Bergerac '89, special reserve, lit a Cuban cigar (the Café des Arts sells some particularly fine ones), puffed and waited to hear what Smiley was so anxious to tell me.

'I have a new work,' he said, blowing smoke into my face. 'A sensitive new work. It has taken me the best part of nine months to complete it.' Smiley was not normally a smoker, though on this occasion, he had invested in a packet of tobacco and some papers. He proceeded to roll several cigarettes and smoke obsessively as he talked.

'Nine months!' scoffed I. Smiley was renowned for having one of the highest turnovers of art in the business. He can usually knock out a painting in about half a day. 'What have you done, given birth?'

Smiley did not acknowledge my joke but bent down and picked up the large leather gladstone bag he once told me had been left to him by a giant forbear. Inside it bore the tooled inscription: He who

laughs last laughs longest. He
placed the bag between us on the table,
disturbing my glass of wine.

'It's in here,' he said grimly. 'And I'd
be grateful if you could take it off my
hands now. I called round at your office
on the way here but it was all locked up.'

'That's because,' I patted him on the
hand. 'I was here, celebrating my good
fortune.' Having drained the last of the
Belgian beer, I lifted the claret bottle high.
'Do join me, please, and drink to the continued success of Humbert, talentless arse-
bandido extraordinaire!'

Smiley looked puzzled for a moment,
frowned his giant's frown as though he
couldn't remember who Humbert was.

This, I thought at the time, was puzzling as they had both attended the Royal College of Art together sometime in the seventies. Not, I had to admit, in one of its finer moments, when every student was producing prize-grabbing works, but you couldn't have everything. Never exactly friends, Humbert and Smiley had always seemed to rub along fairly well. Their work was completely different. Let me sketch them in.

Humbert specialises in what I can only describe as gay porn. He paints acrylics with a trowel, balls and buttocks and beringed nipples; men indulging in the most carnal of acts. Whereas old Smiley explores canine life in delicate oils. Pekes,

pitbulls and poodles are all portrayed in
domestic harmony, draped on chaises, lolling on furs. No hint of genitalia, or
lupine ancestry, his dogs are tame, neu-
tered and they go for a bomb.

Anyway, I digress again. Smiley was
obviously quite agitated. The ginger bum-
fluff on his upper lip (he never managed
to grow a full moustache) was wet with
perspiration and his pale eyes were blood-
shot and protruding. An odd smell exuded from him, a kind of earthy smell
you'd associate with fields of rape or yesterday's sperm. From the gladstone bag
he pulled a black bin liner, which he laid
reverently, almost fearfully upon the table. I guessed that it must conceal the

painting, though to be honest, I was surprised. His work was usually, like himself, on a massive scale. His great danes are life-size, his chihuahuas unnervingly chunky, overflowing the largest of canvasses. He slid his hand inside the bag. I could see its contours lined in black, the huge knuckles, knots of plastic bag.

'I want you to take this painting and destroy it,' he said imperiously. 'We have known each other for many years. I have never asked such a thing of you before but as a friend, I beg you.'

I laid my hand over his in the bin bag, poured him some claret. My heart was beginning to beat quite rapidly. Artists were usually begging me to sell their work, to send it into the stratosphere for posterity. Destruction, especially of a painting by Smiley, was quite against my nature.

'Have a drink,' I commanded, snapping my fingers at the waitress. The punk had begun his second stint of poetry reading. 'It can't be that bad, surely.'

Smiley did not smile. 'Just do as I say. It is the last thing I will ever ask of you.'

He swallowed the glass of wine and unravelled his long legs from under the table. 'I am retiring to my studio. When you have completed the task, please phone and let me know.'

And that was it. he left the painting on the table, retrieved his gladstone bag and loped out of the Café des Arts. I was so anxious to gaze upon his new work that I didn't notice the direction in which he walked.

The punk poet began to shout. He hollered on in a fake Welsh accent about some party he'd been to, how he'd got drunk and drugged and availed himself of some woman he hardly knew. It sounded drearily familiar.

At that moment, I glanced up to see Humbert, obviously having responded to my excited message, prance into the Café, his fuschia fedora at a jaunty angle, his gimlet eyes ringed in black.

'Darling, Mr Aitch!' he exclaimed, clapping me on the back. 'Eight grand, eh? And all for a dwarf with scabs on his nob.

I told you it was only a matter of time!'

The punk poet cleared his throat loudly. All eyes were now upon Humbert and a beastly little new wave verse just couldn't compete.

'Sit down, do, 'I said, snapping my fingers at the waiter again. At least Humbert enjoyed a good red wine. 'And drink to your success.'

'Forty per cent, that's four thousand eight hundred,' he said, grabbing the wine. 'I must say, sweetiepie, you've done the biz this time.'

I shuddered. I cannot bear it when my artists talk about money.

'Enough of that,' I said. 'Let us drink and enjoy the afternoon.'

Humbert sat down. He removed his greatcoat, though the fedora remained in place. This was his image, along with the powder-blue tailcoat and white winged collar. Also, I suspected that his hair was thinning quite alarmingly. He drained his glass and helped himself to another. He picked up the cigar I had ordered for Smiley and ran it under his nose, sniffing in a most disgusting manner.

'You'd not find anything like that on the back streets of Oldham,' he said, leaning over to accept the flame from my lighter. 'I must say, Mr Aitch, honey, you know how to live.'

I too drank deeply. Humbert, everything about him, offended me. He was

a coarse man. Working class. His father had been a factory overseer and his
mother a millgirl when they still had mills.
And worst of all, he was proud of his her-
itage. Often he would seek the grimmer
parts of the north, toilets in parochial bus
stations, cinemas that still showed a cer-
tain type of X-rated film, for his lurid
photographs. His studied campness made
this background all the more incongru-
ous.

'You have done well,' I said to him.
'Let's hope you can keep it up.'

'The world,' he intoned, loudly, 'is
waiting for The Truth -' I never heard
what the truth might be as the punk poet,
annoyed at having been upstaged, stalked

off his podium over to Humbert and punched him in the eye. If it hadn't been for our business relationship, I would have applauded.

After his wound, which was quite considerable, had been seen to by an obliging waitress, and the punk removed from the premises, Humbert fell to disgruntled drinking and muttering. I gathered that although he was pleased at the sale of 'Dwarf with Scab on Nob', he was unhappy that the proceeds would go to an ex wife and child of his, from the time before he had proclaimed his sexuality. The café was filling up with late afternoon drinkers. Many were quite obviously students and smelled of cheap rented accom-

modation and unwashed underwear.
Someone struck up a tune on the guitar, accompanied by a harmonica. The
punk poet stared mournfully through the
window. It had begun to rain. Finally
I remembered Smiley's painting and was
overcome with a desire to see it.

'What the rancid rentboy is that, anyway,' Humbert said suddenly, prodding
the bin bag. He was drinking pink gins
now, never a good sign.

'Your friend, Smiley. It is his new work,'
I said. 'He wants me to bin it.'

Humbert threw his head back so far, he
almost lost his fedora.

'Smiley's no friend of mine,' he mut-
tered. 'I saw him the other day, down

one of those lap dancing places, pleasuring himself all over some poor lass.'

'He is single,' I said, though the comment did confuse me. I had never put Smiley down as the type to frequent that kind of establishment. 'And I'm sure he has needs like the rest of us.'

Humbert slurped his gin pulled the brim of his hat further down over his ears. 'Then he ought to indulge them honestly, not like some rich voyeur.'

I frowned. Humbert was quite obviously drunk. 'So you think the public toilets in parks and bus stations are fair game for finding a lover, whereas a paying club is not. You surprise me, Humbert. And anyway, what were you doing in the lap dancing place if not to indulge your own dubious passions.'

My companion wiped his nose on the back of his hand, tilted his hat over his eyes, lit another of my cigars. 'I followed Smiley,' he said. 'He was dressed up to the nines. I was curious. I have discovered that Smiley is a phoney. He pretends to be some kind of dog-loving family values nut when all the time he's getting his rocks off at expensive porno venues.' He snorted, gathered phlegm in the back of his throat, coughed. I turned away in distaste, began to unwrap Smiley's painting.

'Now, I wonder why he hates this one so much,' I mused, curious as I pulled the painting from its plastic cover. More to the point, I thought, how could I possibly destroy a work by my best selling artist.

'Get a move on, then,' Humbert said, snapping his fingers at the waitress. 'I'm due at the bogs off Orton Alley in fifteen minutes.'

I tutted. I was having difficulty removing the bin bag. The painting still seemed to be wet. A strong smell of linseed oil and turpentine exuded from it. In the background, a riff was struck up on a guitar. A woman set up a wailing, loud and tuneless. The painting slipped from the bag.

'Let's have a decko then,' Humbert shouted. He leaned forward and before I had laid an eye on the work, he had grabbed

it from my hands and turned it around
to face himself. He gazed at it for a few
moments, then spat on it. 'I do not look
like that. I've got more hair for a start.
And my lips are fuller. That tart Smiley
is an utter bitch.'

Incensed, I seized the painting from him
and was shocked to find myself staring
at a portrait of Humbert himself. It was
not a particularly good painting, but neither was it particularly bad. Executed
in thick oil, the brush strokes were broad
and expressive, the face of the sitter, the
artist's own, was somewhat blurred, as
though seen through a distorting lens on
a camera 'No wonder he couldn't stand
the bloody thing,' Humbert said tossing

the painting aside. 'Damned queen's lost the plot. It's out of focus. Unrecognisable. He never could paint people.'

'He can,' I said, outraged at such a slur against the reputation of my best selling artist. 'He is an expressionist.'

'Expressionist my arse,' Humbert sneered. 'You need to learn to paint properly before you deconstruct. Picasso's blue period came a long time afore Cubism. He could paint well before he chose not to. Even Tracey Emin learned to do line drawings at night school.'

'You can hardly compare Smiley with Emin,' I said.

'Nor can you compare that travesty with my face. Look!' Humbert removed his hat to expose his comb-over pate.

We continued in this vein, bickering
madly, slight followed by slight till Humbert, drunk and quite out of control,
picked up the painting and hurled it at
the punk poet who had sneaked back into
the Café and was pointing a water pistol
in the direction of his fedora. The painting felled the poet's mohican. The punk
burst into a Tourretic torrent of abuse. I
drained my final glass of claret, pocketed
my wallet, replaced my fedora, bid the
waitress goodbye and stalked away from
the Café des Arts.

I hope that you, my public, are not ex-
pecting some trite twist in the tail ending
to this masterpiece. Anyone with a mod-

icum of intelligence would have guessed by now that I am Smiley Humbert and Mr Aitch. I sign all my soubriquets with a flourish. I remain mounted and framed, behind glass, preserved for posterity; I cost. My punk poetry is highly sought, bought and distributed.

§ MORE THAN A WOMAN

... ✍

You hardly notice Maria's beard now. A faint golden gleam late in the afternoon, a suggestion of flax upon her upper lip. She has become like so many of her ilk, sad and baggy, flogging the dead horse of an arts course in a mediocre university department threatened with imminent closure. But back then, back in the eighties, her facial hair was a luxuriant affair, a waving tress of gleaming ginger, to be combed and smoothed and stroked. It possessed the rare beauty of the freak show, the stridency of a polemical feminist tract; it hinted at a vulnerable otherness, at once pitied and beloved. I see Maria now and I still want to touch her chin.

'You are a man,' she said

'So I am.'

'What, then are you doing in my gender studies class.'

'I thought that was obvious.'

Silence.

'Studying gender.'

'But you are a man.' And so it went on
until I was compelled to seek the help of
a physician. He gave me a bottle of pills
that made my voice as squeaky as it had
been in my teens. I budded breasts, my
beard fell out.

'I am no longer a man,' I said.

'I can see that.'

'Can I join your class?'

'You are not a woman.'

I stared at her beard.

'Ok. But sit at the back. Any nonsense and you're out.'

Magnificent.

Back then, she became my tutor. The university was in its fading heyday but it had retained some money and some academic prowess. Maria was magnificent. She was not tall, but appeared so. She wore workmen's blue dungarees, the uniform of her sect, along with the doc martin boots, her hair shorn to within an inch of her head. She seemed hard, impenetrable. Her beard swung defiantly between the gentle swell of her unfettered breasts. We all adored her.

'Am I to believe that you are a Marxist?'

'Am I to believe that you are a Feminist?'

'I knew I should never have let a man into the class.'

I, the male oppressor, the white conqueror, gave myself to her. After class, we would sojourn to the pub where she drank pints of ale and pontificated about the struggle, the movement. Her glass ceiling was so well described, I thought I could see the sky on the other side and I wanted to break through and touch it. But more, I wanted to touch her. Although my penis was strapped down, drugged, neglected, in her presence, it became taut with life, a quivering needy thing. I could only look on in awe as she hectored the other tutors, bullied the men, badgered the women, her beard, her badge of office, afire with righteous indignation.

I was a trainee artist on the Fine Arts BA course. It was my final year and to make up the academic requirements, there was a choice between the History of Ceramics, Creative Writing, Gender Studies. There was also a Native American option but the woman who ran that was an acid casualty who had taken a shamanic vow of silence. Gender Studies made up only five per cent of my overall mark but it came to obsess me. From

Pankhurst to Hite, through Greer and
Dworkins, I read, I absorbed. I cancelled
my subscription to the Socialist Worker.
The need for women to attain equality, I
thought, was so much more pressing that
the staid class struggle, which if the min-
ers strike was anything to go by, would
still be around when I was dead and gone.
I took no lovers in my first year at university. Maria had stolen my heart. A
former amor, a young paraplegic, would
call at my bedsit occasionally and find
me in raptures over Simone de Beauvoir.
She would try to cajole me into bed, offering her withered thighs as temptation,
but my head had been turned.

'You've turned right weird since you

started that arty farty stuff,' she accused. 'You've got tits and everything. I don't know why I bother with you. I never wanted a bloke with tits.' This was our last meeting. She wore a basque the same colour as her callipers. It took almost half an hour for her to manoeuvre a sweater back over her head.

How to win Maria became my reason for getting up in the morning. I would lie abed in my damp garret, stroking the mangy fur on my childhood teddy bear and make-believe it was her beard. I would be the first at her class, the last to leave. I devoured her reading list, could quote from the most obscure tracts. My friends deserted me. My art suffered.

One morning, I bumped into Maria coming out of a newsagent, her arms full of Penthouse and Playboy, Reader's Wives, Big 'Uns. She flushed when she saw me, when she saw the size of my own 'uns.

'Carl,' she said,'I hope you don't think these publications are for my own use.'

I hadn't noticed the magazines as much as her beard, freshly laundered but still enticingly peppered with small pieces of muesli.

'Of course not,' I said, automatically. 'The are male propagandist filth, sold to keep women perpetually in chains.'

She nodded and shoved the magazines into a matronly shopping bag, the type my old unfeminist granny took down to the local co op with her.

'Quite right. All the same, I'd rather you didn't mention I bought these. University budgets, you know, the white male supremacist in charge might get a little tetchy.'

She turned on her heels and it was then that I noticed the size of her backside, wondered how I had failed to clock its appetising curves within the denim. The seam on her dungarees was caught between her buttocks, which jostled one another as she walked, rather like two giant haggises caught in straining muslin.

'I love you, Maria,' I shouted into the wind.

Later that week, she was arrested for

ram-raiding a local porn shop; her beautiful beard was snapped on the local news.
If I had owned a video, I couldn't have
replayed that moment more often than I
did in my mind.

It struck me then, that I could do more
to capture my darling's attention than
studying the reading list and mooning
around. I had received a warning from
the art department. If I failed to do any
work in the next half term, I would fail
the course entirely. Art, I thought, could
be the key to her heart. I scouted about,
tried to find out just what sort of art
Maria would part with her heart for. I
should have known. Who but the hand-
somely moustachioed, magnificently mono-

browed Frida Calo would appeal to my
love? Trotsky and Rivera were merely
serendipitous extras. Those harrowing
portraits of fractured bone and bloodied
foetuses; those stern self-portraits of Frida
as roe deer, as splintered column and victim upon the operating table, pierced as
St Sebastian though much, much sexier,
were on display at the city gallery. Maria
made a point of mentioning the exhibi-
tion to me. I was rather hoping she might
ask me to accompany her (we had been
getting on famously, discussing Angela
Carter's **Passion of New Eve** as a masterpiece of ironic feminist tub-thumping)
but she said she'd been three times already and felt moved to tears on each oc-

casion. She said she didn't want me to
see her like that. She touched me then,
lightly upon the arm, sending my heart
into as artistic a swoon as Chatterton's
in Henry Wallis's famous painting. That
evening I returned to my garret and as-
sumed such a pose. There I lay until my
erection, suppressed for so long in the
M&S control girdle I wore to flatten it
down, began to demand attention.

I began painting in earnest, massive
canvases such as the university could still
afford to supply for free, smeared with
my own face, a feminised face, lipsticked,
powdered, positioned above straining
breasts. I painted myself with rabbits,
as an owl, and lastly, most successfully,

giving birth to Charles Handy, American
business guru and champion of women's
rights in the workplace. The trouble was,
that while I was painting all this stuff, the
object of my vehement affections was far
away, in another room, with other people, forgetting me. She was still caught in
that rush of early seventies woman power,
where examining your own vagina with
a speculum was de rigour whereas my
end of year assessment was nigh and I
was in severe danger of failing and being
flung back to the further reaches of the
provinces. Miserable, missing her, I hung
my canvases and waited.

The new Frida paintings did not go
down well in the art department. They

bombed. One old pouff who'd taught there when it was a proper art school, proclaimed them 'essentially monumental but badly rendered'. I could have levelled the same criticism at his boat-race. The director of the course threw a beer glass at me when I entered his office and told me I was crap. I ducked and the glass caught the forehead of an entirely innocent student who was knocked out and had to be taken to Casualty in the boilerman's van.

But all this was as nothing to me. There was only one person I wanted to impress with my paintings. In desperation, I visited her office, an antiquated copy of **Spare Rib** tucked under my arm.

It was late in the day, four-ish, a paltry spring sun leaked through the venetian blinds that were badly in need of a dust. She looked up from her typwriter and our eyes met. I knew then, I knew, that there was more between us than the symbiosis of student and tutor. My now splendid nipples hardened in anticipation.

'Where have you been?' she asked. her voice was slightly breathy, so feminine.

'Working. Come and see.' I despised my new breasts then. I wanted the real thing. Me Tarzan, her Jane. I wanted to be a man again, to make love to this wonderful, unusual woman.

She rose. A strip of sun grazed her beard. My male tool hardened. She took

my hand. In a dream, we navigated the
labyrinthine corridors of the university,
to the Fine Art studios where our nos-
tril twitched, inviting the pungency of oil-
paint and turps, wood shavings, mari-
juana smoke, and old lecturers' urine. We
reached my section of the studio. For
the end of year assessment, it had been
walled off into a secret room, one of my
huge canvases adorned each hardboard
wall. Gallantly, I allowed her to enter
first.

I heard her gasp as she took in the sheer
scale of what I had achieved both in my
paintings and in my body; the rounded
mammaries, the boyish complexion, the
eyes, bright with desire.

'You did all this ... ?'

'For you,' I finished. And we were upon each other. My hungry mouth sought hers, I licked, I sucked, I devoured, my lips prickled from the new sprouted hairs on her beard.

'Darling,' I whispered, struggling frantically to free my penis.

'We can't,' she moaned even as her body arched towards mine.

I tore open her lumberjack's shirt, sending buttons popping over the temporary walls of our haven, was surprised and not a little delighted to find that her breasts were covered in the same wire-textured hair that thrust so joyously from her chin.

'Please, stop,' she begged but it was too late for me. I yanked at her dungarees, they came apart and slipped to her knees, revealing an expanse of flabby muscle, legs so hirsute, a static charge had built up from the nylon in her workclothes.   I bit into those enormous thighs, desperate now to possess her but she pulled away, roughly forced me back, away from her.

'I must have you,' I screamed.. 'I ...'

Maria was weeping, gutteral sobs wracked her walloping great shoulders. Her beard hung, limp, lifeless. The sound of her misery stopped me. I looked up at her from where I was kneeling and there I saw it, obvious to all. Inside the functional Y fronts, was a penis bursting to get out. I shook my head, disbelieving.

'You're a –'

'A man, yes.' Maria began to pull up her trousers.

'But what about the great white chief, the supremacist, the –'

'It was the only way I could get the job. No one wants Gender Studies taught by a man.'

'But isn't that –'

'Sexist, yes. Now, please leave me.'

I did. I returned to the paraplegic whom I later married (and who gave me four bouncing baby boys before wheeling off with the local greengrocer).

There are so many questions I wish I

had asked Maria back then. So many
unanswered clues. Was she really a man,
or a woman on steroids? She obviously
fancied me, so was she gay, straight,
what? I suppose I could ask her now,
now I too am employed by the university, teaching Dog Grooming to under-
graduates, but I won't. I will offer a free
beard-valeting session, perhaps, just so
I can stroke it once more and relive the
good old days before the glass ceiling was
breached by a few birds who feathered
their own nests before replacing it with
weatherproof UPVC.

§ HE AIN'T HEAVY

Sometimes she would moan and ask Jack to cut out the black heart of her but he would only laugh and Nancy would turn over and away from him, try to banish the image of her husband and children. They would rise, unbidden all the same. The cosy fireside, memories shared and she would say to him 'I am an adulteress.' Just the word made her feel exotic, dangerous. Jack told her that he did not care for guilt or self-pity. He was a jack-the-lad. Freedom oozed from his pores. Nancy would lick his hairline and taste and smell it: an unfamiliar and strange scent.

But it was he whose heart had given

out while her black ventricles still
pumped and thudded. He was astride her
when it happened. The first time in her
conjugal bed, an afternoon sneaked between school sports and hometime. The
shopping done, tea in the oven, a sum-
mer day in early July. He clutched at his
chest in the way soap actors do when an
overblown character is blown away. She
laughed and jiggled her hips. Dark spit-
tle oozed from his lips. He was inside
her, hard and sure. She contracted her
muscles, milked him to death. But what
a death. If it wasn't so unfortunate, him
being on top of her like this, she would see
the funny side. It was an urban myth, a
story from a woman's magazine. It was

a joke. She could hear the lads down the pub, her husband one of them: 'Lucky bugger. I wouldn't mind going like that.'

Except the poor bugger, her lover, her jack-the lad is dead and lying on top of her and inside of her, his full twelve stone squashing the breath out of her, his full seven inches engorged and pressing up towards her cervix and showing no signs of deflation. She lies there, staring at the crack in the ceiling, the crack that her husband fears is a sign of subsidence, the crack she stares at when her husband pushes her onto her back and pumps away for three minutes or so before rolling off into sleep. She smells the shepherd's pie in the oven and hopes she put in on a medium heat. She wonders what food they will serve at her lover's funeral and how many women will be there. Her eyeballs, the only part of her anatomy she can move comfortably, swivel in her head, search for something to fix her attention on. She squirms beneath him and jerks her hips but they are stuck fast as dogs in the street, end to end.

Nancy closes her eyes. Sun dappled shade plays beneath her lids. She wonders if she could sleep like this, if she would be found later, peacefully aslumber as a princess in a fairy tale, waiting to be woken by... By whom? Her prince, the cause and the keeper of her sleep, is dead. Where to go now in a narrative that must maintain a forward thrust, resisting the past at all costs. She wonders if she will be seen as the victim or the perpetrator of the crime for which she will surely pay. She considers a feminist take — not the outdated bra-burning stand she learned at college in the eighties but a new post-modern, media-driven irony about the female condition. She decides quickly, that it cannot help her any more than Germaine and her cronies could all those years ago. Does she, Nancy, have a responsibility to clean up her own story by failing to mention any history that may sway the listener into believing that adultery can be understood if not condoned — or will the mere fact that Jack

has pegged out in the way he has be seen
as judgement enough?

Sleep is coming.   She feels relaxed,
warm, despite the rapid cooling of her
lover's body. She waits for grief to set
in with rigor mortis and is surprised to
find that she is neither upset nor relieved,
maybe because the gruesome fact of the
situation, that her lover is dead, has not
yet hit in any but an intellectual way.
She can still feel him inside her, could if
she wanted, probably achieve an orgasm,
but even the tabloids, even deconstructed
post-modern feminists would probably
balk at necrophilia, so instead she con-
tents herself with opening her eyes and
straining around to look at the window,

which is half open, the off-white linen curtains blowing in scents of geranium and rose.

After some time, she has no way of guessing how much as the clock is under the bed where it fell during their passionate coitus, she is aware of a shadow passing through the room, a sudden coldness descending. Jack's once golden skin has developed a pale blue cast and there is a new smell overriding the scents of sex. It is a sweet, rotten smell, somewhere between the rose petal water she made as a child, and decaying meat.

Downstairs, the telephone rings, a few seconds later the doorbell. Something pecks and taps at the window. The cur-

tains blow in with a sudden whoosh. She
hears the key turning in the front door,
her husband returning home early from
work? The room is filled with black wings,
a cawing, a flapping and she believes that
this is the end, the final judgement upon
herself and her misdeeds, that there is to
be no ambiguity after all. A crow circles
the ceiling, coming to land, then posing
magnificently upon the brass bedstead,
inches away from Nancy's toe. She shud-
ders, revolted yet thrilled by the seeming
malevolence of the creature. Jack's dead
body gasps, belches and for a moment
she is deceived into thinking that maybe
he isn't dead at all, just sleeping or col-
lapsed. His cock, with the force of all that

last escaped air, shrinks, pulls away a little and again she attempts escape but the dead weight of him pins her to the bed. She peers over his marbling shoulder and finds the crow staring at her unblinkingly, it's hard black little claws holding tight to the bed frame.

'Go, you horrible thing,' she shouts, trying to move herself, her body to make it leave. 'Get out.'

It caws as if in answer, coolly surveys her and her predicament. Nancy claws at Jack's back, panicked now. The thing could peck out her eyes, leave her with this dead thing, blind and helpless. She feels her heart flutter, beat against her ribcage. There are footsteps on the stairs.

The crow raises itself, puffs out its sleek black chest, extends it's raggedy wings.

'Bernard!' Nancy shouts, screams her husband's name. The door to their bedroom, the bedroom they have shared for over twenty years, bursts open in a way that could have been farcical in a less equivocal tale. Over the top of Jack's dead head and the crow's tattered wings, she can't see anything, though it is clear that someone has entered the room. She remembers her underwear, soiled and sodden on the floor near the door, wonders vaguely if her husband will trip over it. She bellows out his name, the breath escaping from her in short, blustery bursts. 'Bernard, Bernard, help me!'

Now the crow wants out. It extends its wings, rises to the ceiling, plunges downwards in a horrifying attack against the intruder.

The intruder is now getting what Nancy had worried were her just deserts. The bird is lunging at him, pecking wildly. Blood spatters the peach anaglypta. She feels, in her paralysed state, a most exquisite sense of terror and pity, for herself and her husband.

'Bernard,' she says quietly, in the way she might speak his name if they were sitting, thigh to thigh, on the sofa downstairs watching a film. He screams in reply. Jack's body erupts again, more gasses, this time foul-smelling escape from his anus. The bird leaves its victim, wheels around the room, flapping madly. It seems intent, suddenly, on the bed and its unfortunate occupants.

'Bernard?'

A hand clutches at the sheets, her husband's hand, familiar and dear. She wishes she could console it.

Even the relentless, no-flashback forward pace of the narrative cannot eradicate all sense of moral ambiguity. For the sake of others, for their immortal souls, she acknowledges her culpability by giving her dead Jack-the-lad a kiss on the shoulder. She has no compunction about doing this in front of her husband as his eyes have been removed by the crow and he can only thrash blindly about the entwined bodies. And anyway, in this story at least, where he only gets the walk-on cuckold role, his soul is safe as houses. She sighs, stares up at the crack in the ceiling, a convenient hook in the arc of the story, a suitable place to leave this amoral, **immoral** woman thinking maybe it was subsidence, maybe and maybe Jack will tear out her black heart after all.

§ DOWN THE CHIP SHOP

God, him being a writer is an aphrodisiac at first. He may not be as hirsute as Mr Armitage but he can spout poetry which is short and amusing, though not in an affected way. And he's had quite a lot of it published. He reads books, which is something your dead-from-the-neck-up-husband never did. And not just biographies either, but proper novels with a plot you can discuss, characters you can really get to grips with. And you can spend your time screwing and laughing and thanking your lucky stars that at last you've found someone with a decent sized hard drive.

There are some flies in the ointment.

Your husband is not going to lie down and
accept you and his kids living round the
corner with your new bloke. When you
file for divorce, he goes ape, keeps phon-
ing and threatening and accusing you of
taking stuff from the house you once
shared, like the Punjabi medal his grand-
father won in some war or other, and a
bayonet he bought twenty years ago, at
a car boot. He demands to know how
much the new bloke earns, puts a detec-
tive on the case, discovers that he earns
bugger-all, he's a writer, after all, a poet
who lives on the dole. This makes your
husband temporarily smug but long-term
furious. He suspects you and the bard
have plotted it all, that you intend to

rob him of his lifetime's achievement: his house, his few trinkets, his collection of women's underwear, sized eighteen. You were never interested in that stuff, though, were you. Not money, not anything materialistic though you like a drink. You like good food and trips to the theatre. You're a writer too, after all and you're above talking about anything so mundane as money.

Anyway, to get back to the romance, which is going strong, you have so much in common! Intertext and intercourse, plot and sub plot. God, it's good. You read each other's work in bed, though deny this to writer friends who sneer. But then your poet starts giving you more of

his stuff to read. He gets annoyed if you
read anything by anyone else. On the
bedside table lies a teetering pile of un-
read novels. You used to love novels. You
ate them, according to your mother who
only reads the Daily Mail and quotes it
at you any time you're together. His un-
published and published works run to a
lifetime's collection for anyone else and
he's still only forty odd. He's got books
and books of short stories, of poetry. And
then there are the novels, the novellas,
the experimental plays. You climb into
bed at 12, exhausted after work and he's
there, ready for some fiction action, his
eyes bright as he hands you yet another
manuscript. 'You'll really like this one,'

he says excitedly. 'This is a work of pure genius.' You laugh and think he's joking but pretty soon you realise he's not. So, you turn over in bed and start the first page. You're tired, the words swim in front of your eyes. You yawn. He's immediately up demanding to know if you're finding it boring. He's pointing out phrases he thinks are particularly good, reciting in the monotonous monotone he uses at public readings. You agree, they are good. You desperately want to sleep.

In the morning, his erection is enormous. He's been dreaming, he says, of being interviewed by Melvin Bragg. No, he's not being interviewed, you have been invited to a posthumous celebration of his

life. He says that in the dream Melvin's
hair is as luxuriant as ever, though his
teeth look false. He must be seventy if
he's a day, you say, buying time. Your
poet ignores this. 'You'll be talking over
my latest work, he says, thrusting another manuscript under your nose. His
cock is tickling your undercarriage but
you're too tired to care. 'Have a read of
this, darling and let me know what you
think.' Now he's entering you. You start
to read, again. It's touch and go whether
your orgasm is more important to him
than you finishing his book. You see your
own name, feel sick wondering what the
hell you'll say to old Melvin.

This new piece, the piece Melvin will

be going on about is ostentatiously au-
tobiographical. It is a novel about his
sexual conquests. He hasn't even both-
ered changing the names. The characters, their jobs, even their addresses are
there in black and white for any weirdo to
read. Your mobile number is down there
too, as well as the landline. You read on.

The phone goes. Your son answers for
in this version of your life you have a son,
not just a daughter. You have three children in fact which makes your ex-husband
even more furious that they've been stolen
by the poet. It is, of course, your ex on
the phone now. He wants the kids for the
weekend and as far as you're concerned,
he's welcome. You could do with a day

in bed, a week if the truth be known.
Your eyes are gone with all the reading
and you wonder about booking an ap-
pointment with the optician. You say yes
about the kids then realise too late what
this will mean. You see, in your mind's
eye, your writer lover sneaking up behind
you, bending you over, giving you another stack of manuscripts to praise while
he slips you a length.

'How you getting on with the poet,
then?' your ex demands. His voice grates
and you wonder how you put up with him
long enough to conceive and deliver the
three kids.

'Great,' you say, inwardly debating
whether this is a lie or not. You know you

sound tired, that this will please your ex
who refuses to leave you alone even since
you moved out of his house.

Anyway, there's the current work of genius to consider. You're not even on page
two and its scaring the hell out of you.
When you get back into bed to read, you
notice that your beloved is perusing a
book by someone else. This annoys you
slightly but with the best will in the world,
three fictional kids and a poorly paid part
time job don't leave you much time to
attempt an output as great as his. And
to give him his due, he has read most
of your sorry portfolio, all you have to
show for fifteen years graft. He's reading
a book by a serial womaniser, an Amer-

ican guy who lives to write, who shags and boozes and does little else. You begin to worry that your man sees him as an inspiration, that you are just one of the fun-for-a-while-women in his writer's life, that his new work is a thinly disguised homage. But you haven't got time to worry about trivialities like the future, like whether you've picked a potboiler of a man or just some slim volume with literary pretensions. You have too much to bloody read.

On page two your worst fears are confirmed. Not only is your character in his book really you, with your name, address and history, but he's got you shacked up with him and boozing too much and on the dole. You are mad as hell. God you haven't had a drop since Saturday and now its Tuesday and you work. You decide that if he's put the kids in the book as well you'll ask him to move out. Then he turns you over and kisses you and your start to feel vaguely randy so the big showdown is left till later.

Later in the day, he's gone out to the library. Research he says, for his latest masterpiece. For once you've a day off work, the children are with their embittered father and the computer is free. You sit down and start to write a revenge book. You put the poet in it, warts and all. And he did have warts once, he told you. Round his arse. He probably doesn't realise but there's still one there, hanging down like a parson's nose on a chicken. You've never mentioned it but put it in the book on page three, add a couple of venereal diseases to his history, then take them out because you're only fuelling his deluded literary construct of the macho man.

His latest tome, the one about the women is on the computer table as you write and occasionally you open it at a page and smile. You smile because his take on the women in his life is so very different from what you know to be the reality. His parade of leggy brunettes, sensuous Indians, orgasmic Orientals is really a sorry freak show. He admits every time he is drunk that the women in his life before you all seemed to possess some grotesque defect. One had webbed feet, one had been circumcised; one had lost most of her hair. There was a grossly overweight one, a grossly underweight one with a massive vagina, a hirsute German with a mat of pubic hair. One Bulgarian had a wooden leg and there was a slender Dane with a glass eye. His real life women had more attachments than a vacuum cleaner. Sometimes you wonder if it was the flaws that attracted him, that if this is the case, then you must have one yourself. This thought has preoccupied you for some time. Often you find yourself studying your toes, teeth and tonsils. You have examined your nether regions with a shaving mirror and you cannot pass a shop window without having a quick look. Could your bulky calves have attracted him, the stretch marks on your thighs? Or maybe it is your poor anus, buggered in your early twenties by a man of unnatural proportions, left somewhat worse for wear.

But you have a great afternoon, celebrate starting your new work by cracking open the bottle of chablis you've been keeping for your first anniversary. You press the save button on your PC and savour your wine.

He returns from the library with a stack of books, two of which are his own. He was so pleased to have found them there that he got them out on his ticket. You remind him that he has about forty copies of each, that the publisher had to remainder the hardback edition but he is not to be deterred. He also tells you, that he has defaced twelve copies of a rival poet's work he found next to his own. He joins you with the wine, goes out to get more. By the fourth bottle, you're feeling rather tiddly. You attempt a blow job and demand to know if you're more accomplished than the woman with no teeth. He doesn't reply, just shakes his John Thomas and stalks over to the computer, says he going to work for a while and could you hurry up and finish his book, tell him what you think.

Your ex phones again. All the children
have got nits, he tells you. He has got
nits on his head and in his pubes. He
bought some insecticide shampoo but its
given him a rash on his cock. He accuses
you of neglecting the children.

You go to bed, pick up a book of poetry
by your lover, fall asleep.

The explosion erupts at midnight.

'What the hell is this?' It is the poet,
naked, ranting. He has discovered your
new work, all the undisguised truths, all
his women nailed to his hard drive in your
story.

His poetry collection has stuck to
your sweating face, you are still drunk

and had been in a deep sleep. You spot a
nit leaping about on the hairs in his chest.
You realise that this is one of the turning
points of the story. The end of Act Two
in a play. There will be a race to the end
and you know you should have sewn the
seeds of plot earlier but there is no plot,
or maybe there are two in conflict with
one another and that is the conflict in the
story. There is the plot of your ex and the
kids and you being with the poet per se
and then there is the other more urgent
problem of your poet and the book you've
begun about him and the way he expects
you to read everything he has written and
shag him several times a day as well as
keeping up the job and looking after the

fictional kids. At this point you have to
make a decision, do you carry on with
your story, finish it off, keep to the truth
as you see it, or do you sanitise, get rid
of the warts, and the nits.

Your poet lover is angry but he is also
tumescent. His cock glistens, it bends
gently to the left. Lice frolic in his pubic hair. You peel his poetry from your
face, turn around, thrust your buttocks
towards him. Your history is always fiction. The kids are with their father.
There is always the delete key. A sonnet
is a small price to pay.

§ FLESH

W e had him now, Fat Boy cornered at the edge of the field. Naked he was, and cowering, pressed back into the winter hawthorn. Fifteen of us running, shotguns cocked. Maia ran beside me, six foot of gym-fit golden brown, her hair blowing in the breeze behind her.

'Let him go,' she screamed. You know what they'll do -'

I knew. The hunt pressed on. I ran out ahead. He was within my reach. For a moment, our eyes locked. My bayonet was centimeters from his chest. I shook my head gently. 'Run.' Fat boy gave a last whelp then dove under the hedgerow. We saw the domes of his luminous but-

tocks, the sturdy pillars of his milk-white
legs, his upturned feet, brown with mud
and human soil. Then he was gone. His
pale form was seen running, stumbling
across the top field and into the woods
beyond.

'He'll get picked up on the Tod road,'
I said. 'They sent a mob out there, over
near Croxley's old place. We'd better get
going.'

Maia bent down, her hands on her knees.
'Can't. I'm winded.'

Surprised, I stared at her. Maia was
one of the strongest. She'd trained as
a dancer since she was three and never
stopped moving. Behind us, the rest were
turning to leave. I waved them off, thir-

teen lithe bodies running with the grace of deer. 'I let the poor bastard go. What happens now isn't your responsibility. Come on, what's up?'

Maia glanced at me, smiled wanly. 'I am pregnant. We should have known, I guess. But I'm not sorry, though I know it means things will have to change between us.' She began to cough, her shoulders heaved. Vomit spewed from her mouth.

I closed my eyes, willing it not to be true, took her hand, helping her to stand, and brushed a rogue strand of hair from her eyes. 'You okay, now?'

She nodded, though she was clearly unwell. 'It's due in spring.'

We had discussed the possibility, of course we had. But we had always been careful, bought prophylactics on the black market, using the withdrawal method if necessary.

'Lawrence?' she said.

'What?' My voice was gruff, almost aggressive.

She sighed and looked away. 'It doesn't matter.'

I knew what she wanted but it could not happen. We would never be a unit, Maia and I and our unborn child.

Fat Boy escaped. The hunters on the Tod Road were too busy organizing themselves to see an eighteen stone mound of flesh thunder past them until it was too late. And it had begun to rain. You had to hand it to some of these lard-arses, they were quick enough on their feet, even in the kind of weather that sent the rest of us running for cover.

I left Maia in the village outside the Juice 'n' Oxygen bar, wondering if it would be the last I saw of her. We couldn't embrace, not publicly, had to content ourselves with the merest brush of fingertips. The baby wasn't showing yet but once the authorities got wind, then she'd be bundled away to the maternity home until she'd got rid of every gram of baby fat and was fit to be seen again. It wasn't always like this. I dimly remembered my mother's form rounding as my brother grew inside her. Twenty years ago, she was allowed into food stores and shopping malls at any time of day and people didn't try and hide her away.

I walked through the village, located my car outside the leisure centre. I had planned to go for a swim and a game of squash after the hunt, but Maia's news and the sudden memory of my mother had dampened my mood. A storm was brewing, the temperature had dropped and rain lashed my waxed jacket. I straightened my shoulders. Was this how it started, the apathy that lead to obesity? I climbed into the passenger seat and switched on the engine. I had almost used my fuel quota for the month

and the gauge was flashing. I leaned my
head on the steering wheel, blinked away
tears. It was about time the affair with
Maia came to an end.

Home was over twenty kilometers away,
on the outskirts of the city. I had bought
the cabin when interest rates were rela-
tively low. Since then, the war had caused
property to rocket and all of my salary
from the magazine went into the mort-
gage. I lived in constant fear of debt,
of eviction and the workhouse. I sighed,
started up the engine and set the dials for
home. If it hadn't been for my sordid secret, I would have sold up and moved out
into the sticks where prices were still af-
fordable. I dozed as the car sped through

the countryside. It was a dark day, late
November and a mist was already steal-
ing over the fields. Approaching the city,
I could see the high-rise cabin towers loom-
ing up over older buildings, the cranes
and scaffolding cluttering the skyline. My
cabin was located in an up and coming
area. A row of semi detached houses were
bulldozed to make way for the building
and traces of the old suburban road remained, though fortunately, nothing of
the the poor immigrants, its later inhab-
itants.

The car ran into its port and stopped.

'Hey, Lawrie, howabout chess, tonight?
We haven't played in ages.' This was
Chico, rapping on the car window. He

lived in the next cabin to mine. I waited a moment, glad of the darkness, collecting my thoughts before sliding open the door.

'No. Not tonight, thanks,' I said, guiltily. Chico and I used to be good friends.

'Still working for the Consummate Consumer, Flesh? The only way I get to hear your views these days is to buy that rag.'

I faked light-heartedness, switched the car to sleep mode. 'Believe me, Chico. They are not my views.'

We walked together to the lift. Chico was telling me about his job for the environment minister. As usual, the news was all doom and gloom and exploding populations but I was glad to avoid more intimate subjects. 'Anyway, how's Gabrielle?' he asked eventually, as the lift pinged to the nineteenth floor. 'It is so long since Stella and I saw you both. Why don't you come over for supper one evening? Nothing too formal. We can do a couple of circuits in the gym to wear it off, after.'

'Great.' I avoided Chico's friendly eye.

We left the lift in silence, but as I turned to enter my cabin, Chico clapped me on the shoulder. 'Listen, mate. I can help. Whatever's going on between you and Gabrielle, can be resolved. And if it's money -'

'Everything's fine, thanks.' I blinked at the camera and my door slid open.

Gabrielle, my sordid secret. The reason why Maia and Chico and every other friend had now to be repulsed. Supine, she waited on the ancient king-sized bed. Black satin sheets, rumpled up, watermarked with sweat. The faux tiger skin rug had fallen to the floor. Gabrielle was naked, unable to find clothes to fit her. She slept fitfully day and night. Her blonde hair was damp, plastered around her cherubic face and mascara ran from the corners of her eyes to her chin, giving her a strange, tribal appearance.

'Darling,' this said with a muffled sob.

'Hi.' I slung my briefcase on the floor beside the bed and sat down. The bed took up the entire living space, more or

less. The wall-bunks were unreachable.
We had thought the bed such fun when
we first got together. The time we spent
in the cabin was for sleeping and making
love only, we reasoned. For the rest, we
were working or in the gym or canteen. It
didn't matter that the cabin was the bed.
Now I would have given a year's salary to
be rid of it.

'What you been up to?' I asked, gazing
with dismay at the wrappers, the plates,
the evidence of gorging out of control.

'The usual.' She gave a bleak little
smile. 'My options are rather limited.'

I tutted, forced myself to look at her.

'And you?' she asked.

I thought of the hunt, the exhilaration

of racing through the fields, Maia's news.
'Oh, the usual.'

Gabrielle turned. There was a smear
of faeces on her inner thigh. 'I waited for
so long. I rang the magazine. They said
you weren't in today.'

I tried to stop my face from flushing.
'Sorry, had a story to cover, down near
New Mill ...'

'You were with her weren't you?' There
was no real accusation in her voice, only
resignation.

I busied myself, tidying up the debris.
'I was with a lot of people. There was
a hunt, though the guy must have been
pretty fit. He gave us the slip.

'What was his weight?' She always

asked this, just to torture herself.

'Oh, who cares,' I feigned boredom. 'Eighteen, nineteen. I don't know.'

She began to weep. I felt the anger building up in me again, wished I had gone to the gym instead of straight home. The air was foetid, thick and sweet, smelling of sweat and confectionery and shit, and something else, something female, hormonal, as though a permanently on-heat animal lived there. And the cabin was so hot. Gabrielle had the thermostat set to max, though she knew the environmental cost.

'I care,' she wailed. 'You, my life-mate, writes for the most influential publication in the state. Flesh is not just a mirror

of our society, it actually influences it.
These ... these hunts. Flesh hunts. You
must take some **responsibility** ... '

I edged my way around the bed, forced
myself to look at her. Every day it gave
me a shock. Gabrielle was twenty-four,
twenty-five stones. The mass of her dim-
pled flesh spread across the mattress;
lumpen legs, huge lolling breasts, a stomach that folded itself into geographical
mounds. She was unable to wipe the excrement from her own backside. She was
unable to even get into the shower room.
One of my daily tasks was to empty and
disinfect the buckets in which she defe-
cated and pissed, my other to shred the
evidence of her overeating, to get it into

the waste disposal after midnight when
everyone in the cabin block had bedded
down. If I was caught ...

It didn't bear thinking about.

'I can't legislate for the mob,' I said,
bitterly. 'Nor can I do anything about the
housing crisis, about jobs, the collapse of
welfare ... All I can do –'

'Is print pretty pictures of thin beautiful women, diet advice, exercise regimes,
advertise slimming drugs and laxatives.
All you can do is hunt down another poor
bastard who weighs more than you -'

'Shut up!' I yelled. I longed to strike
her, could almost feel the pleasant ring
of my hand hitting her face. But things
in our relationship had taken an atavis-

tic turn as it was, without me resorting to violence. I took a few deep breaths. 'Look,' I said, forcing myself to remain calm, 'If it wasn't for **Flesh** then you and I wouldn't have a bloody roof over our heads, or we'd have to live somewhere a little more ... public. As it is people are wondering about you.'

Who?'

I told her about Chico's offer of supper. She sighed and wiped away a few more self pitying tears. I filled a bucket with warm soapy water and began to sponge her over. I knew little of animal husbandry but felt then like a last-century farmer washing down a beast.

'Did you bring my ...' she began.

I shook my head impatiently. I had not thought of food since Maia's news.

'You've been out all day and never gave me a thought,' she whined. You must have passed three, four supermarkets. Where was the hunt. I can't believe — '

'I'll go out again,' I said.

'Too late.' She indicted the clock on the computer screen. 'Another of Flesh's bright ideas, wasn't it? Shut all food stores after six, then people won't be tempted to eat late. Along with the purchase limit and tax on carbohydrate and fat –'

'Will you keep your voice down?' I whispered, thinking of Chico in the next cabin. The walls were so thin, we could hear him and Stella making love some nights. As it was he had guessed there was a problem and I didn't want to fuel his suspicions. I couldn't risk anyone calling round.

I'll just have to sort myself out, won't I? She pushed me away, although I had not yet removed the shit on her thigh, brought up the Food-Mart site on screen and typed her order. I stumbled into the shower and remained for half an hour under the hot, cleansing spray; wishing, remembering.

Once Gabrielle was beautiful: blonde, green-eyed, athletic. We were a beautiful couple. I was rising star of **Flesh**, she was my muse, my cover girl, a fitness instructor discovered in a gym in

the fashionable city centre. Together we
could take on the world. Or that's how
it seemed to me. I should have spotted
the signs; her refusal to allow me to meet
her parents or to tell me her real name. It
took months of research to trace her identity. When I did, I was sorry I'd both-
ered. Her folks were trash, living in a
trailer at some docks out east. Her father had been banged up for embezzle-
ment, her mother was so fat, her stomach was banded. Gabrielle was their only
child. I deleted the file and concentrated
on the woman I loved. Together we chose
the cabin, decorated it, bought the old
fashioned bed. Together. We thought it
would last forever.

The boxes started arriving shortly after Gabrielle lost our first child. She miscarried in her sixth week, before we had told anyone. At first, she seemed fine. Christmas was on the way and she spent hours on the web, choosing gifts for my many nieces and nephews. The boxes continued after Christmas and well into the New Year. By the end of January, it was clear that Gabrielle was suffering from some kind of mental collapse. They piled up in the hallway outside our front door. I heaved them into the cabin, ripped open packets of sushi and salad, low-fat milkshakes and ready-made meals. I wanted to call a doctor, get her checked out, but she stopped me. 'It's normal,' she insisted. So I allowed her to swell.

She became pregnant again, soon after. This time, she managed to hold on to it for four months and had already moved into the massive state maternity home when the bleeding started again. She was allowed home three days later and the over-eating began in earnest. There were three more miscarriages, the second two remained unreported. Gabrielle's weight began to increase. She stopped going into work and was sacked over the web. She began to lie in bed all day, eating or staring hopelessly at the ceiling.

At the same time, my career was on the up. I'd been promoted and now had three other journalists working under me. My reports were quoted all over the media, my weekly column considered a litmus to the zeitgeist. It helped to concentrate on work and not think about Gabrielle and our dead babies. My time was divided between the office and the gym. I met Maia, began the affair. Gabrielle became less and less important, her ballooning form occupying the smallest portion of my consciousness. Such hypocrisy. Hungry readers fed upon my homages to youth and health while my wife gorged on misery, boxed with extra fries.

The hunt idea started as a joke in the August issue of **Flesh**. With the extinction of the old targets, fox and hare, I suggested the pro-hunting lobby go af-

ter fatties instead. The Rustic Alliance
took it seriously and, by October, portly
people all over the land were in jeopardy
from waxed-jacketed skinnies with their
packs of horses and hounds. It began as
a joke. When caught, the unfortunate
prey were photographed and allowed to
go free. Some were given lifetime memberships to health and diet clubs. Others became celebrities in their own right,
publicly battling the bulge with the en-
couragement of a starving audience. But
my readers wanted blood, not fat. The
first death occurred the following January. The hounds ripped a man's heart
out while the hunters bayed; he was still
warm. Now it was a free for all, vicious,

bloodthirsty, corrupt; overtaking football in popularity. The latest was to spit-roast the obese, hang them over a fire and watch them turn into crackling. Some joke. And it was all done in my name. Lawrence McKrie, the man holding the health of the nation in the palm of his well honed hand. Posters of me were pasted over every billboard on the free-way. Lawrence McKrie: **The Voice** of **Flesh**.

If only they knew.

I switched off the shower and grabbed a towel. The doorbell went. Gabrielle's order. I slung on my robe, pulled the hood low down on my face and un- locked the door. Gabrielle rolled to the far side of the bed where she wouldn't be seen.

'Four burgers, eight fries. Double cheese pizza with pepperoni, fruit of the forest gateau, three bars choc –'

'Okay.' At first I didn't look up. The guys who delivered that shit were as guilty as those who ordered it. The trade in illegal food would stay healthy so long as everyone kept their mouths shut and respected each other's anonymity. I took the boxes from him, getting a waft of grease and dough. 'How much?' He took out the bill. It was then I noticed how fat he was. Hands like sausages. A wedding ring digging deep in the pink flesh. I looked up into the very same face I had spared this morning.

'No!' He dropped the boxes on the

floor and stared at me. Gabrielle slith-
ered across the bed to retrieve them. 'You
are so -' He clocked her, her size, the
black silk, the shit I had missed on her
leg. So Fat Boy had a job. And what a
job, delivering fat food to fat women. I
should have let the mob at him while I
had the chance.

I spent the night worrying. How much
had he seen? Would he risk the wrath of
the hunt by informing on me. Would they
come after Gabrielle, or me? I took another shower, tried to remove any traces
of Fat Boy's touch. I shared a pizza with
Gabrielle, perched on the bed beside her,
trembling with indignation, fury and fear.

'What's wrong? she asked, her lips trembling.

I couldn't tell her. If I admitted letting him go, she would think I was on her side, condoning the obese, as though I thought it was okay to pig out night after night. As though pizza and burgers and chips, chips, chips were good for her. Later on, we made love but her soft folds provided little comfort. She fell asleep sobbing into the grease -stained sheets.

Nothing happened. Nothing worse than that. Next day, in the office of Flesh, I set up a centrefold spread with Tonya Richards, the so-called fittest woman in the state. The war was going badly; things were hotting up in the West. It was good to have such an attractive diversion.

Two months went by and I began to relax. Fat Boy had run scared, or maybe he remembered the kindness I had done him on the hunt field and spared me. Maybe he didn't realise what was at stake. Gabrielle, too, appeared to forget. She even seemed a little happier, began to lose some weight. Some nights she didn't eat the food I bought for her and spent hours surfing the web. Some nights she enfolded me in her soft flesh and I felt something of the old desire.

Not that I needed to. Tonya Richards had quickly yielded to my charms. I missed Maia, of course I did, and thought often about her, how my child must be growing inside of her. But Tonya was hot,

young, and so grateful for her escape from
the old east. War and famine had eaten
her state, leaving a barren waste and a
few, scattered starving orphans. She was
so grateful to me for her extended visa
that she allowed me to take her with in-
creasing ferociousness. I wanted to possess, to devour her. We ate out every
night, Indian, Chinese, Sushi. She blind-
folded me, fed me quality chocolates. She
made sure everything we ate was made
from fresh legal ingredients. It was a nov-
elty for me to indulge my so appetites
fully. I had never known food to taste
this good, nor a woman so greedy for me.

Two months stolen from time.

Cover story in the Picton Times: Maia

Goldberg, famous beauty, found in state care. A picture of my former lover, naked, evidently pregnant, her well toned skin stretched into a tanned dome. She lay on a bed draped in black satin. I couldn't help but think of Gabrielle. I scanned the story. There was some hypothesizing about the identity of the child's father. My name was mentioned as well as half a dozen others. I didn't read further than page one.

The next day, the backlash began. We should have seen it coming. For some time, I had been receiving a trickle of letters from overweight people complaining that they were being misrepresented in my magazine. The trickle became an avalanche. Our offices were boycotted. A hunt in the south was sabotaged by lardies. Three slender women, shoppers, were mown down in the Capital by an "unidentified mess of flesh". The gloves were off.

Exactly two months from the day Chico had asked me to supper, I arrived back at the cabin early, to find him ensconced with Stella and Gabrielle on the king sized bed, munching away on some fast food junk. I was horrified. Chico had always kept himself trim though he must have been a good ten years older than me. And Stella, who was still a size six, wouldn't have been seen dead eating such crap at one time.

'You're never in at this time,' Gabrielle

said evenly, when I accused them of violating the law. 'Out with whatshername Richards. We do this once a week. You never usually come back here.'

I was dumbfounded, not only by the food and the fact that Chico evidently enjoyed the company of my grotesque wife, but also by the calmness with which Gabrielle proclaimed her knowledge of my affair with Tonya. I thought we'd been very discreet. But then she passed me a copy of the Picton. Inside, my sexual antics had been entertaining the populous for several weeks. I was only glad these exposés seemed to have escaped attention from my colleagues at Flesh.

'The return of Free Choice', the headline screamed, next day. 'Eat what you will'. We held an emergency meeting at Flesh. The main backer talked about folding, starting up some new project: Fast Food Fitness. They wanted me as editor. I didn't have the stomach for it.

'We stand our ground,' I said. 'The Roman Hunt is on next week. Every fat bastard in the state will be locking themselves in ...' I paused, remembering Gabrielle cowering in the cabin. I'd promised to take the day off to protect her, but now my career was on the line. 'We'll cover it in detail, bring out a special issue. I've got Tonya bare-back riding across the moors for the cover. The senate are still pro hunting. The public are on our side.'

'The public!'   One of the directors pushed the current health figures across the table. 'The gap between rich and poor, enlightened and not, is growing again.   We've got celebs wearing retro **Burger King** tee shirts, there's a charity ball next month, big do, **everyone** will be there. And what's on the menu? Bloody Big Mac and chips and Mayo to go on the side!'

I was defiant. 'Then the coverage of the Roman Hunt will have to blow them out of the water.' Who can we get?'

They went along with me. They had no choice. I was 'The Voice,' after all. They had to listen.   In truth, I could barely stand the sound of my own utterances.

On the morning of the Roman Hunt, I kissed Gabrielle with more passion than usual, reminded her to keep hidden. Briefly, she held me close; my head squashed into her massive breasts.

'I'm sorry,' she whispered.

'I know,' I extricated myself, wiped butter from my chin.

I got to work and assembled my arsenal: Eighteen emaciated soap stars, TV and still cameras every fifty metres, two helicopters off-loading ticker tape offering free memberships to gyms and health clubs. With the backing of the Senate, we'd commandeered ninety percent of the state airwaves. My employers had nothing to fear. **Flesh** would soon be at the head of the pack; thin the flavour of the month again.

The hunt was to start right there, in the middle of the city. After all, this had become an urban issue. I'd hired horses, a whole cavalry of them, invited every diet junky I could find to come along and try their hand at hunting down a fatty. I stepped out of the office, onto the steps. Two hundred scarlet coated individuals pranced along the street. The riders were drinking warm smoothies, mineral water. The beagles bayed, pulled on their leads, their breath billowing. It was the most exciting sight. I lifted the horn to my lips and blew.

Slow motion. We galloped out of the

town, down streets deserted of cars but lined with people screaming and waving rattles. I was at the forefront, amid the dogs. Behind me I could hear the pounding of hundreds of hooves, the whooping of the delighted crowd. Beside me, Tonya astride a silver mare, her red hair flowing. The January air was icy, sharp. The sky a crystalline blue. Out of the town towards the ever diminishing green belt.

Then I saw him. Fat Boy. Naked as the day he was born, belting along the Tod Road in a weird repeat of the November Hunt. I should have known. I blew the horn. The dogs went crazy. Fat Boy leapt the fence into the same field we'd cornered him before. Tonya screamed.

From nowhere, two forms appeared, two
visions they seemed then. I was riding
into the low winter sun, half blinded. I
was good on a horse, but not that good;
thrown at the fence Fat Boy had jumped
so easily. The hounds began to howl. I
felt their hot slavering breath before their
teeth. 'Not me,' I shouted. 'Not me. Go
after the fat boy.' A foot upon my shoulder. High heel, dominatrix style. I looked
up into Gabrielle's face, unrecognisable,
so different from the way she had seemed
that morning. Black leather, thigh boots.
Some fetish madam from the last century.

'Got him.' She was wheeling a lasso in
the air, now a cowgirl from some movie.
I still hadn't worked it out. Then Maia

appeared, her body huge but beautiful, fertile, her skin rosy. She looked more alive than I had ever seen her. I gazed up at her rounded stomach and felt my own contract in awe. Gabrielle had wanted a child so much. She too, placed a high-heeled foot upon my squirming torso, digging the toe into my spleen. Then Tonya was down from her horse, pulling the horn from where it was clipped at my belt. She put it to her lips.

'Wait,' I screamed. 'What are you doing?'

'This will put Flesh ahead of the game,' Fat Boy said. 'Their senior editor fed to the hounds. At least he won't get fat.' He'd procured a camera from a trash-bin, slung it around his neck so it bumped against his naked stomach as he walked. He aimed the lens at me and Gabrielle's foot ground into my collar-bone. 'This is for your devoted readers, Lawrence'.

A chill wind blew. My colleagues from the magazine surrounded me, snapping cameras, taking notes. The dogs were pulled off and tethered. I could hear the crowd shouting my name, the impatient stamp of the horses. Gabrielle stood over me, a bayonet in her hand as I writhed in the mud of the field. 'Cold are you?' She pushed it into my chest and I passed out.

I can smell fast food, that fatty, greasy stench of the old time burger van. Tonya is with me, stroking my face. I feel hot, so hot. Flames lick around my chest. There are so many people watching, my women, my friends, my colleagues. My hands and feet are bound, the heat is unbearable. Fat Boy bastes me in oil. Slowly, I am cooking.

'This is for Flesh, your flesh; Flesh of your flesh,' Fat Boy said. Maia rubbed in the salt. I smelt so good.